BIGGEST LITTLE HEART

STARWOOD CHRONICLES, BOOK FOUR-CLEAN, SWEET SMALL TOWN ROMANCE

BOBBY HUTCHINSON

1

————

"**M**orning, Doctor Murphy."

The check-out girl at Overwaitea gave Colin a huge smile.

He smiled back and glanced down at her name tag as she clicked in the price of his bread, peanut butter, milk and canned tuna.

"How's it going, Rosa?" He ought to have known her name, the girl had been checking out his groceries since he'd started the locum in Starwood three weeks ago.

"Great, Doctor. Did you find everything you needed this morning?"

"Yes, I did, thank you kindly."

The question was tiresome, but he was always polite. They were obviously taught to ask it at every checkout, and it was good for him, because it reminded him of an irascible elderly woman patient who'd snapped at him last week when he automatically said, "And how are you today, Mrs. Simons?" while studying her file.

"How the hell do you think I am? I'm here to see you, Doctor, and I'm sick, that's how I am, or I wouldn't be wasting your time

and my own. So, stop asking dumbass questions and get on with it."

That had smartened him up, all right. He grinned at the memory, and Rosa gave him a flirtatious little smile and turned pink.

"That's twenty-three forty, doctor."

He had his card out to pay when a small girl tugged at his pantleg, holding up the car keys he must have dropped when he pulled out his wallet.

"Well, thank you—" he glanced at the grinning little girl again. "Why bless me, it's Lily. I do thank you, Lily." He turned to search for her mother.

Joanne Logan was two customers back, baby Zalika over her shoulder, five-year-old Alex holding on to the cart.

"Hi, Colin." Joanne used a finger to push up her huge red glasses, hazel eyes twinkling. Her wide smile and spikey blonde hair emphasized her heart-shaped face; as always, Colin thought how lovely she was.

Beautiful, just. Her smile was like sunshine, and it had always brightened his day.

"Joanne, great to see you." She'd been in his office with Zalika just once since he moved here, but he'd often seen Joanne and the baby at the pediatric surgical ward in Calgary.

Colin had scrubbed in when the pediatric surgeon operated on tiny Zalika's heart a few months ago. He could still picture the minuscule brown baby attached to tubes and surrounded by white-coated surgeons fighting to save her life. She'd only just arrived from Nigeria.

Joanne had been there when the wee mite was taken into the surgical suite, and she was waiting anxiously when the operation was over. Then she'd stayed close beside Zalika during those first few crucial days. Joanne was only a temporary foster mother who'd been called in at the last minute, and he'd been amazed at her dedication to the tiny girl.

He remembered the powerful jolt of physical awareness he'd felt when he first met Joanne, a visceral attraction that had increased the more he got to know her.

She was attractive in an offbeat fashion that intrigued him. Sure, she was an exceptional foster mother. But it was the woman with the deep, contagious giggle, the expressive eyes, the lush, full breasts and ample hips that haunted his dreams.

He glanced at Zalika, plump and smiling, one hand tugging at Joanne's red glasses, and then his gaze returned to the woman holding the tiny lass.

Joanne. He'd met her that first day and gradually gotten to know her in the following weeks.

She'd had to drive back and forth to Calgary over and over for Zalika's appointments, making arrangements for someone to run her daycare business and mind her other two kids. It couldn't have been easy, for certain.

He'd tried to have even a few moments to talk with her, gradually getting to know her better and better over an occasional coffee and several hurried cafeteria luncheons.

He'd learned that she was divorced, that she loved children, that she had none of her own due to some problem.

That first day, Colin and the other surgeons had thought it likely the wee baby wouldn't survive, but she had. She'd flourished. It had been what his own Irish mother would label a God-given miracle, one that came down to a mother's love. Joanne's love.

Colin had asked to scrub in when he heard about the case, because of the complexity of the operation and his own passionate interest in pediatric surgery, but afterwards, it had been as much Joanne as her new foster daughter that intrigued him.

He wondered if the lovely woman had any idea that his presence in Starwood had everything to do with his wanting to see more of her, away from the hospital. He wanted to get to know her in a personal, and he scarcely dared to hope, in an intimate way. Given time.

And that was impossible to do with him in Calgary finishing up his residency, and Joanne here running a busy daycare and taking care of her little brood.

When he'd spotted the notice asking for a doc to do a locum in Starwood, he'd leapt at the chance only because she lived here.

Starwood wasn't exactly the bustling metropolis where he'd always imagined practicing medicine. But the clinic was surprisingly busy and the patients interesting; having five coal mines in the area made for a variety of challenging cases due to accidents. And he went on hoping that before very long, he and Joanne would really connect.

He'd asked her to join him for lunch one day soon after he'd arrived, but then an emergency had forced him to cancel. And when he asked her again, it was her duties as a daycare provider that had prevented their meeting.

He longed to ask her right now, here in Overwaitea, to have lunch today, but he was driving back to Calgary later this morning for a meeting, and he wouldn't be back until the following morning. But when he got back, he was going to make certain that luncheon happened.

In fact, he'd just pick up a funny card in a few minutes at the drugstore and drop it in her mailbox on his way out of town, that he would. And in it, he'd ask her to go out with him.

He felt pleased with himself, planning something like

that. One of the women he'd dated had once accused him of not having a romantic bone in his body.

So there now, Nora it was. Or was it Margaret? The lass's name had escaped him, but he thought he could be as romantic as the next fellow. It all had to do with incentives.

Nothing ventured, nothing gained, his father had always said. It was one of the few things the old drunken reprobate had ever said that made any sense. Whatever good genes and common-sense Colin had inherited had come from Molly, his mother.

God rest her soul.

She'd died three months after Colin's med school graduation in Dublin, and he was forever grateful she'd been able to attend. She'd bequeathed him his love of healing, had Molly, and his love of all children as well as his deep respect for women.

In many ways, Joanne reminded him of his mother.

2

———

Joanne loaded her groceries on the counter, watching out of the corner of her eye as the tall, gangling doctor with the charming Irish brogue walked out of the store.

She'd always thought he had the loveliest deep blue eyes, unusual with that unkempt curly black hair. Thick long eyelashes as well. No wonder he'd caused a stir among Starwood's single women when he came to work at the Medical Centre, and they learned he wasn't married or involved with anyone.

He needed a haircut; he always seemed to need a haircut. He had great shoulders and a nice ass, and an endearingly crooked nose. And he was four years older than her 38; she'd been curious enough to check him out on the web long ago, after a lunch they shared at Calgary Hospital.

Not that she had any designs on him, she assured herself. She'd vowed after the divorce she'd devote her entire life to children, her foster children and the others she cared for daily.

There was something broken in her, something that

made it impossible to carry babies to term or to sustain a relationship.

Nope, she had no designs on Colin Murphy. He was sweet and kind and gentle, though. And if she was in the market for a relationship, those were traits she'd put at the top of her list.

She smiled to herself because Colin was unaware that his white tee shirt was inside out.

During their many encounters at the hospital in Calgary, she noticed that he paid no attention to how he looked or what he was wearing.

Twice, he'd had different coloured socks. Once, his trainers didn't match; one was blue, the other brown. Several times he'd had smears of food all down his front. And he dropped things constantly, like the keys that Lily had retrieved just now. It was appealing. And he'd always been so caring, kind to her and Zalika, and warm and responsive to Lily and Alex.

She'd suspected he was maybe a bit attracted to her, and when he came here to Starwood and asked her out, she was convinced of it. It was flattering, having a man ask her to lunch, even though it had never worked out yet with Colin —and never would.

Who in their right mind would take on a woman with three kids, one of whom needed extensive medical treatment and would for many years to come? Especially a woman with a track record like hers of bad decisions, miscarriages, stillbirth and divorce. The familiar painful feelings welled up in her, guilt, failure, bad choices, deep sadness and despair for her lost babies.

"We going to the lib'ry now, mommy?"

Alex was helping her load the groceries on the conveyor,

and she forced the bad feelings away and smiled down at him, tousling his thick brown hair.

Her beautiful boy. Her beautiful family. She'd been fostering for three years, Alex since he was two and Lily from just before she turned a year old. She'd applied to adopt both of them and, of course, Zalika as well. But being a single woman with a limited income was making it extra difficult, and Alex's birth mother couldn't be located to sign the necessary papers.

"Let's get these groceries to the car, and then we have to go straight to daycare. We can't have the other kids waiting for us, can we?" She'd had Timothy come in early just so she could do this big grocery shop, but even though he was terrific with the kids, she didn't want to leave him too long alone.

The library was wheelchair friendly, and he was adept at moving around on his crutches. Still, a gaggle of two and three-year-olds challenged even a non-disabled person as they all headed off in different directions to find whatever mischief they could.

Timothy had lost his right leg above the knee in a motorcycle accident and he was being fitted for a new prosthetic, but it was a slow process. The one he had chafed badly, forcing him to use crutches and the wheelchair more often than he wanted. The daycare had reached the point where she needed a full-time assistant. Once the new leg was ready, she'd take him on full-time.

She felt blessed to work with kids and earn a decent living at it. She felt blessed to have found an assistant like Timothy. He'd come from a family of nine, one of the eldest, so he had lots of experience. He was funny, imaginative, and loving, fantastic with the little ones, able to soothe even the most fractious among them.

With her small helpers impeding her at every turn, she loaded the groceries in the car and headed off to the Starwood library, where she leased the three basement rooms that made up Tiny Tots Daycare.

"Hey, Jo—you're just in time." Timothy was relieved. "Mabel had a smelly accident, and I need to change her. But I didn't want to leave these other rascals for even a few moments. They must have had too much sugar for breakfast this morning."

He scooped up stinky two-year-old Mabel onto his knee, impervious to the foul odour coming from her diaper, and headed to the washroom, singing, "Row, row, row your boat—."

Joanne shoved the perishables in the fridge, comforted Amanda, settled Zalika in a cot for a nap, handed out juice and slices of apple, stopped Jeremy from hammering Louis with a toy umbrella, and generally settled in for the typical day of chaos, diapers, laughter, tears and hefty doses of love.

By six P.M., most of the little ones had been picked up. Besides her own three, only five-year-old Susie and her four-year-old foster brother Marcus were left.

Joanne was both tired and exhilarated. She no longer felt like she'd lost part of her soul when the last child headed out the door. That terrible feeling was gone now that she had three lovely children to foster and shower with love.

Years before, the only time she'd been around children was when she ran the preschooler program in the summer. Then, as now, she loved chasing after the tiny hooligans all day.

And then, just like now, they'd return to their natural families at the end of the day. And back then, she'd have to go home to an empty house, empty of children, devoid of love, and soon enough, bereft of a husband too.

Lars had moved out when she lost the last baby girl she'd named Angelica. She'd begged him after that to adopt or at least foster.

He'd refused. "I can't go on like this, Joanne, this hoping and waiting and losing," he'd said. "I want kids before I get much older, my kids, not some throwaway leftovers of someone else's. And it's pretty clear that isn't going to happen with you."

His cruel words had cut like glass into her heart.

3

———

Lars had remarried within a month of their divorce and thankfully, moved to Vancouver so she didn't have to see him every time she turned around. Starwood was a small town.

And typical of the gossipy place, she'd learned soon after he left that he'd been having an affair with the girl he married. And she *was* a girl, barely twenty. They had two kids now, and Joanne wished them well.

Now that she had three tiny humans to care for, the awful lost feeling was only an occasional memory, like poking a tooth that used to ache. Her therapist had likened her guttural reaction to PTSD.

"It's a perfectly natural response," Dr. Hill had explained. "Losing two babies early in pregnancy and then one full term causes emotional wounds that take time to heal."

She wasn't entirely over losing those babies; she never would be. But she was undoubtedly better. None of the medications prescribed for her had ever comforted her the way the children did. Her two daughters and her son were her best medicine.

"C'mon, gang, let's get rolling." Joanne was dropping Marcus and Susie off at The Biggest Little Truckstop, the thriving restaurant their parents owned.

Kate, Susie's mom and a good friend had insisted that Joanne not go to all that trouble. She said that she could run over quickly and get Susie; the Truckstop was almost next door to the library.

But Joanne won out because the restaurant was right on her way home anyway, and she knew how crazy busy the place got every Tuesday and Thursday afternoon.

Those were the two days when the specials were half-price with a coupon, and the new dishes the chefs Jamie and Mac were trying were often served free as tasters. There was always a lineup, and today was no different.

Joanne herded her brood to the kitchen door, glad she didn't have to elbow her way through the crowd in front.

"Hand delivery," she yelled into the controlled chaos of the Truckstop kitchen.

She was carrying Zalika while Susie and Lily were hanging on to her pants, giggling and pretending she was an airplane. Alex, who at five felt he was far too old to be so silly, marched along behind them. Marcus, who hero-worshipped Alex and did everything he did, copied his friend right down to the serious expression on his face.

"You are a saint," Kate hurried over, and Susie wrapped herself around her mother.

"Mommy, mommy, look what I made for you." She held out the picture, coloured cheerios arranged like a rainbow.

"That's totally awesome, Susie. We'll put it up on the fridge at home. What did you make, Marcus?" Kate knelt and hugged her daughter, reaching out to include Marcus. But the boy squirmed away.

Kate and Mac had gone to Ontario to bring Marcus home with them, but Marcus still had problems fitting in. He still desperately missed his mother, Kate's cousin, who'd died five months before. He often asked when his real mother was coming to get him, which was hard on Kate.

Kate and Joanne had had many long conversations about fostering. It had made their friendship even stronger and more profound.

"Sorry I couldn't keep them longer today; the social worker's coming," Joanne apologized.

She usually babysat Susie and Marcus for a few hours extra on busy days at the restaurant. She didn't mind, and her kids loved playing with the other two. Susie adored Zalika and Lily, and the boys played well together. "Tomorrow for sure—"

"Don't you even go there," Kate warned. "Wait a sec."

She went to the fridge and then handed Joanne a size-able insulated bag. "Mac made you that Miner's Meat Pie you like, and there's Mac and Cheese for the kids. And some Coal Dust Cookies for dessert."

"Kate, there's no need..." Joanne started, but Kate dismissed her protest with a wave of her hand. "It's the absolute least we can do. You've been such a big help with Susie and Marcus."

"Small payback for all the times you and Edna took my two when Zalika was in the hospital."

Edna was Kate's sister-in-law. She'd recently had her own baby boy, and the three women supported one another.

"Now I need to be straight with you," Joanne went on in a severe tone, and then had to giggle at the alarm on her friend's face. "It's all been done with the most selfish intent. We *love* hanging out with Susie, don't we, girls?"

Lily shrieked in agreement, and the baby held her arms out to Susie and began to giggle when Susie hugged her. "These fine gentlemen keep the ladies in order, right, boys?"

Marcus and Alex were too busy watching Mac put meringue on lemon pies to respond. He held out spoons and let them lick the last of the lemon filling out of the huge bowl.

Joanne checked her wristwatch. "Need to get going. Thanks for the food, Kate and Mac. You have no idea how much I appreciate it." Especially today. It meant she could feed the kids when she got in the door at home instead of making them wait while she prepared something healthy.

And today, of all days, that was a huge bonus.

4

———

Once they were in the car Alex leaned over and looked at the bag on the floor.

"We got Mac and Cheese, mommy?"

"We sure do."

"And *cookies,*" he crooned.

"Yes, honey. But we can't have them in the car," Joanne replied.

"No dirty car." Bossy Lily shook her little finger at her brother and scowled at him. He simply nodded and smiled at her.

It always surprised Joanne just how gentle and understanding Alex was with his sisters, even when they seemed to join forces to drive him crazy.

"Mommy, park?" Lily asked while they were driving past Starwood's water park.

Zalika also pointed her finger towards the swings and sucked on her pacifier with vigour, kicking her skinny little brown legs against her car seat.

"I wish we could, but Mrs. White is coming to visit us

today, remember?" Joanne felt the anxious knot in her stomach pull tighter.

The social worker's visits were expected, and the older woman was always encouraging and positive. Still, Joanne knew it was Mrs. White's reports that decided whether or not she'd get final approval for adoption.

"We give some cookies to Mrs. White, Mommy?" Alex asked.

Joanne was sure that the little boy was a genius. He knew exactly what would get him what he wanted from each person. The kid would make a fine psychologist; she smiled to herself. And Mrs. White had a sweet tooth.

Joanne had explained to the kids that they needed to be honest and always answer Mrs. White's questions when she came to visit because she was there to make sure that Joanne was a good mommy to them.

The first and last time she'd ever seen Alex throw a total screaming fit was when he asked whether Mrs. White could take them away from her, and Joanne had to begin her long-winded explanation with, " Yes, but—."

He'd been sick to his stomach from all the crying.

Deep down, Joanne knew they would never find a reason to take her kids away because she would never give them one. She was a model foster mother. And most of the young working parents in Starwood trusted her with their children. There was always a waiting list at Tiny Tots.

But still, every time they had a scheduled visit from Social Services, Joanne felt on the inside the scared way Alex had looked that day he'd thrown his only tantrum.

Joanne pulled into the driveway of her renovated miner's cottage. The cottages had been built in the early 1900s for underground workers and their families, and Joanne had scraped up enough for a small down payment after her divorce, using the money from the sale of the more modern house she and Lars had been living in.

Although her cottage was anything but upscale, it suited her perfectly.

Square and simple, sturdy wood construction with grey asphalt siding and a red roof, the cottage was two stories high. A small entrance porch led into a kitchen, pantry, a tiny living room, and an even tinier room miner's wives had called "the parlour." That parlour had been kept pristine and reserved for unique visitors, but Joanne had turned it into a playroom for the kids.

Upstairs were three small bedrooms and a bathroom, an added convenience that the original cottage hadn't had; the so-called "necessary" had been an outhouse in the spacious back garden where there was now a set of swings and a small playhouse.

The front of the house had a narrow flower bed that came within a few feet of the sidewalk, and Joanne had planted geraniums and snapdragons, two flowers the mule deer didn't devour.

The deer roamed freely through Starwood, eating almost everything residents tried to grow, and Joanne had added generously to their diet until she found the few species of flowers they didn't eat.

"Look, mommy, we got's mail," Lily squealed.

She'd installed one of those old-timey mailboxes with the red flag on the side. She'd thought it'd be fun for the kids to see the flag up, but she also loved it.

Or she used to before medical bills and notices from Children's Services made her less enthusiastic. Today there was only one envelope, a purple one with no stamp, no return address and her name in big, loopy letters.

How strange. She tossed the envelope on the hall table

for later. She longed to open it right away, but Mrs. White was always prompt, and there was just enough time left to feed the kids and give the house a last-minute tidy.

And just when she had gotten everything and everyone in order, she heard the knock at the door. It was one of the weird quirks that Mrs. White had. Never in the years she'd been visiting Joanne had she ever rung the doorbell.

Joanne pasted a smile on her face and checked herself in the hallway mirror. She didn't look half as exhausted and anxious as she felt. She'd washed her face and put on a fresh shirt and jeans.

Perfect. She pushed her glasses up her nose and opened the door.

Her smile quickly faded when she saw Mrs. White's severe and concerned expression. She usually was smiling, her delicate features reflecting the kind person she was, but today Joanne could tell that something was bothering the plump little woman.

As usual, Mrs. White greeted the kids first in the small playroom. Zalika was in her playpen, and the other two were watching cartoons and enjoying their cookies.

Then Joanne led the way into the kitchen, where she'd set out tea and what was left of the cookies.

"What is it, Mrs. White? Please come in here and tell me." Her heart was hammering, and she could feel perspiration gathering under her arms.

"I just hate to be the bearer of bad news, but there's an issue with Zalika's papers," Mrs. White said. "I'm so sorry, Joanne. Because the citizenship issue hasn't been resolved, the authorities are refusing to renew her Visa."

And instantly, Joanne felt the world fall apart right underneath her feet.

5

───────

"I'm sure we'll figure something out," Mrs. White said, patting Joanne on the back. "There's still time before they send her back to Nigeria. And we aren't going to let that happen."

"She can't go back; she just can't. What about her heart problems?" Joanne agonized, staring blankly at the cookies untouched on the table in front of them.

When Zalika's first Canadian adoption fell through, authorities scrambled to find a placement for her because of her life-threatening heart condition. She was already in Canada, a bonus, and Joanne was approved as a first-class caregiver and foster mother.

So, after a series of convoluted screw-ups and delays on the part of the immigration department, Zalika had come to live with Joanne as a temporary foster child, even before everything was in order and official.

Joanne instantly fell in love and applied to adopt the sweet baby.

Zalika had a temporary Visa, and child services had assured Joanne that by the time it expired, they'd have the official citizenship status settled for the baby, and formal adoption procedures could proceed.

"We are *not* going to let her be sent back," Mrs. White said.

"But, you can't be totally certain, can you?"

Mrs. White gave Joanne a sympathetic look and then slowly shook her head. "I've been doing this job for almost thirty years, and unfortunately I've seen this scenario play out many times. Legal issues are a problem for all sorts of reasons, and expired or rejected Visas are one of them. Especially with children from foreign countries, third world countries, like Nigeria."

She stirred three spoonfuls of sugar into the tea Joanne had poured. "Rest assured, I'll be doing everything I can to ensure Zalika stays right where she belongs, here with you. But we need to be prepared for the worst. There are simply no guarantees."

"What more can I possibly do? What would make a difference?" Joanne's hand trembled as she offered the cookies.

Mrs. White nibbled at a cookie and sipped her tea. "Zalika's heart condition was the reason the rules were bent. It's a miracle how she's recovered the way she has, but her health can no longer be used as a reason to extend the Visa."

Joanne stared at the other woman. "You're saying that if she still had severe medical issues, there wouldn't be a problem?" The very idea made her feel sick. She'd celebrated every small victory in the baby's recovery, and now ironically, her good health was endangering her.

Mrs. White sighed and nodded. "Terrible as it sounds, that's probably true. And, of course, there's the issue of you being a single parent with no ties to Nigeria."

"There's nothing I can do about that. No one else has come forward to adopt Zalika, have they?"

Mrs. White shook her head. "No, they haven't. The previous adoption fell through because the mother had terminal cancer."

"And if she were sent back, she'd be placed in some atrocious orphanage. Chances are good she wouldn't survive."

Joanne was on the verge of tears.

Mrs. White got to her feet. "I have to be on my way, Joanne. I'm so very sorry about all this."

Not as sorry as I am, Joanne thought as she stood at the door and watched the social worker drive away.

There had to be a way, there just had to be.

6

There was no time to dwell on her own problems, however. In the playroom, Zalika was fussing. It was past her bedtime. And that, in turn, was making Lily whiney.

Alex, too, was overtired. He was complaining about some toy he wanted to play with that he couldn't find.

The kids' moods seemed to always go down in a domino effect. Joanne felt despondent and desperate, but she didn't want her kids to sense that anything was wrong. She forced a smile and scooped the baby up.

"Come on, Lily, let's get your sister cleaned up and into bed and then we'll have time for stories."

The trick to getting Zalika to sleep without protests was as simple as a bath. And the lavender-scented baby wash also helped the tiny girl to settle.

As Joanne was gently massaging the soft, squishy arms of this precious baby girl, she felt a sob well up. She swallowed it and forced a smile instead as she washed Zalika's body from her sweet little toes to her dark, curly hair.

Incision scars, needle marks, and defibrillator burns

plagued the skin on the baby's fragile chest. She'd suffered her first heart attack at just four weeks old. The doctors in the Nigerian hospital where she'd been born and lived for the first couple of months of her life had little to work with.

They'd had to shock her with a regular-sized defibrillator as they didn't have one for babies. She was a fighter. It was a miracle that she'd survived until she was brought to Canada.

And I'll fight for you with every breath in my body, Joanne promised after drying Zalika off and putting her into her soft flannel pyjamas, then tucking the baby in her crib.

Once Zalika was asleep, Alex and Lily had a bit of tv time to unwind, and then they were also taken to bed. Joanne read them two stories each and kissed them goodnight.

She checked on Zalika once more, poured a glass of white wine, curled up on the couch, and finally allowed herself to cry. She felt as if she was being punished, constantly losing babies, one way or the other.

Punishment. It was what she'd felt when she lost the babies. She'd been a wild child in her late teens and early twenties. She'd been mixed up with some questionable and dangerous people in Calgary.

She'd fallen hard for Brad, a bartender at the club where she waitressed, and she'd gotten pregnant by him. He'd pressured her to have an abortion, and she went through with it.

Afterwards, the full impact of what she'd done hit her, and it had been the incentive for changing her life. She'd left Brad, gone back to school, and taken early childhood education and the other courses necessary to qualify as a child care supervisor.

She'd met Lars, a carpenter, and they'd gotten married.

She'd never told him about the abortion, but she'd always felt that losing her babies with Lars was punishment for that horrific mistake. She'd regretted it all these years, agonizing over it, praying for forgiveness.

She'd never intentionally hurt anyone else—only herself and that tiny unborn baby. And all that was so very long ago before she was married. Did she have to do penance for the rest of her life for that one teenage mistake?

She sipped the wine, blew her nose and took the glass into the kitchen. The purple envelope lay on the narrow table in the entrance hall. She tore it open.

The card inside had a lush lady in a purple tutu reclining on a chaise longue, wine glass in hand. The caption read, *"Some people are just born Fabulous!"*

It made her smile. She wiped away the last of the tears and flipped it open.

"So, Ms. Fabulous, would you consider having dinner with me? Name the time; I'll arrange the place. I'll be waiting anxiously for your call. My cell--250-425-0733

Hopefully,

Colin."

A thrill shot through her.

And suddenly, she knew what she had to do.

7

————

"Joanne?"

Colin answered immediately. "Ahhhh, so you have the card, Joanne. And is this to be my lucky day?"

His soft Irish brogue, his deep voice, made her hesitate. There was such hope in his tone. She nearly lost her nerve.

"I—I would love to have dinner with you, but that's not why I'm calling." She had to clear her throat. "There's—there's something I need to discuss with you, Colin. In person." She couldn't explain it on the phone; she needed to see him. "As—as soon as possible?"

"Of course, of course. I'm in Calgary just now, Joanne. But I'll be back early in the morning. Could we meet then?"

"Oh, I'm so sorry to bother you." Suddenly she was embarrassed.

"You're never a bother," he said softly. "It's not the wee one, is it, Joanne? She's not having problems?"

It was about Zalika, but not the way he meant it.

"Zalika's fine. I—I need to talk to you."

"Are you alright, Joanne?" he asked, the urgency returning to his voice.

"I'm—I'm okay." *Not really.*

"Do you think we could meet? I need to talk to you."

"What is it about?"

"I'd rather not say over the phone," Joanne swallowed hard. "But I need a favour. A big one."

"Let's get a coffee tomorrow morning. I'll call you the minute I get back."

"Thank you, Colin."

"See you tomorrow morning," he said and hung up.

Joanne made herself tea. She curled up on the couch and sipped it, trying to plan exactly what to say to Colin. At midnight she went to bed, tossing and turning, unable to sleep.

When her cell phone rang, Joanne stared at her bedside clock. Six-fifteen in the morning. She struggled up and tried to sound awake. She must have finally dozed off.

"Hi, Colin. Wow, you did mean early. Did you drive half the night?"

"Sorry to wake you, but I'm due to start my shift at the hospital at 8, so I left Calgary before dawn. I'm concerned about you, Joanne. You sounded very upset last night. Can we meet soon? I'm driving, still about a half hour away."

"For sure. I just need to wake the kids and--"

"I can come by your house," Colin said, and then he paused for a bit. "If that'd be more convenient for you."

Joanne didn't usually have a lot of people over. She talked openly to Kate and Edna, but not many others. She was an absolute wizard with kids, but she wasn't all too trusting when it came to adults, with a few exceptions of course.

Maybe it was because she didn't want to get too close to

anyone, even as a friend because then she'd have to open up about her miscarriages and how much they had broken her inside. Starwood was a small town, so people knew some stuff but not everything.

"Sure, I'll have coffee on," Joanne said after a short pause. It was perfect, really. The house would give them the privacy they needed for that critical conversation.

She checked on the kids, who were still fast asleep. With a start, she realized that this was the first time that Zalika had slept all through the night.

Joanne smiled down at the little girl. Why did she need to make this even more difficult than it already was by being the perfect baby?

She put the coffee on, took a quick shower, and prepared cereal and fruit for the kids. They usually woke up around 7:30. She'd park them in front of the TV with their breakfasts, so hopefully, she and Colin wouldn't have too many interruptions.

She'd just poured her first cup of coffee when Colin arrived. He didn't knock or ring the bell. He texted instead, *At the door, can I come in?*

"I didn't want to wake the kids in case they were still asleep," he said softly when Joanne opened the door.

"Good thinking," Joanne smiled up at him. His deep blue eyes were clear and alert, his hair rumpled and curling as usual on his neck. "You don't look like you've been travelling half the night," she said, grabbing a mug and pouring coffee for him.

He was wearing jeans and a blue tee that matched his eyes. It had a brown stain on the front.

"I'm very used to early mornings and sleepless nights. Being an intern trains a fellow to get by on a minimum of sleep."

She remembered that when Zalika was in the hospital in Calgary, Colin would often come in and talk to her early in the morning or very late at night.

If she'd been at a different stage in her life, she'd have quickly fallen in love with him then, warm and compassionate and caring as he was. And great to look at into the bargain. But she was not in the market for a relationship; she reminded herself. Not then, not now.

She placed the coffee cups on the table and sat just across from him. She hoped he wouldn't notice that her hands were trembling.

"So, what's going on?" he said when she didn't speak for a while.

She drew in a breath and let it go in a rush. "Zalika's Visa is about to expire, and they are not going to renew it. They'll send her back to Nigeria and put her in some dreadful orphanage." Her eyes welled up, and she pushed her glasses out of the way and wiped away the tears with a tissue.

Damn, she'd promised herself she wouldn't cry.

"I'm so sorry, Joanne. Is there anything I can do?"

He reached across and put one of his long-fingered hands on hers. His skin was warm, his touch comforting. His blue eyes were filled with concern.

"There might be." Joanne lifted her eyes and looked right into Colin's. He urged her on with a nod.

"She got a temporary Visa for medical reasons; you remember that, Colin. So, I'm thinking that maybe she could get it renewed for medical reasons."

He gave her a puzzled look. "But Zalika's been doing great lately. Her latest tests were excellent. She's caught up with other babies her age, which is remarkable. And Child Services are proceeding with your adoption application, aren't they?"

"The adoption hasn't been approved yet." Joanne paused. "There's not much I can do about that. But if somehow it looked as if Zalika's health had deteriorated a bit..."

Colin's eyes narrowed. "You're asking me to falsify her medical records?"

"It would mean she could stay in Canada. With me, with her family." Joanne suddenly recognized the enormity of what she was asking.

Colin slowly took his hand away from hers. "Joanne, I understand how desperate you feel. If there were anything legal I could do to help, I'd gladly do it. But what you're asking would put my career on the line. I could lose my license."

"Hi mommy." Lily bounced into the kitchen holding her teddy bear tight against her body, a thumb in her mouth. She gave Colin a shy smile and he reached out and rumpled her hair.

"Morning, lovely Lily." His voice was gentle and sad.

Joanne took the sleepy girl into her arms, gathered up one of the breakfast bowls she'd prepared and carried her daughter into the living room. She turned the TV on and searched for a kid's program. The enormity of what she'd asked Colin to do was registering, and she felt horribly ashamed of herself.

When she returned to the kitchen, Colin was on his feet.

"I'm going to see if there's anything I can legally do to help you, Joanne. But I worked too hard and long to endanger my license. I'm sorry."

"Colin, please..." Joanne walked up to him, but he took a big step back and lifted up a hand.

"I admire you more than you know. I'd like to get to know you better, I'm very attracted to you. But in spite of my feelings for you, I can't risk my license," he said in a low voice.

"I'm sorry, Colin. I shouldn't have asked. It's just that I can't lose Zalika, I can't let them send her back." Joanne took a step towards him again, but he shook his head and went out the door.

Joanne felt frozen, unable to move. She'd made a terrible, selfish mistake. She'd destroyed whatever there might have been between herself and a good, kind man, a man she now realized might actually have someday loved her.

She saw the lovely card on the cupboard, and she read it again, every word tearing a hole in her heart.

She'd blown it. Why did everything she tried to do turn to dust?

A crippling sense of loneliness, an awareness of how much she longed, on some level, for a man to share her love and her children, immobilized her.

She saw again the hurt in Colin's eyes, in his tone, and it made her shudder. She wanted nothing more than to crawl into a hole and stay there for the rest of her miserable life.

The sound of her baby waking was what eventually got through to her. She had kids to care for. She had a daycare to run. She couldn't fall apart, too many people were counting on her.

Zalika was counting on her, even though the baby wasn't aware of it. She had to put her own feelings on hold and concentrate on finding another way to help her little girl.

There was one more avenue to explore, much as she hated to go there.

But she'd have to make a trip to Calgary, it couldn't be done over the phone.

8

———

Joanne ran the only daycare in Starwood, so it was always difficult to find someone to take over managing it, even for a day.

She rarely needed to go anywhere, but right now she was a woman with a mission that couldn't even wait for her next half-day off.

Timothy was a great assistant, but his missing leg meant he couldn't deal with the kids all on his own for an entire day, so Joanne had been taking off two mornings a week instead of a whole day. The coalmines worked twenty-four-seven all year long, so there were kids needing care every day of the week.

Mac's sister Edna had helped out before, and Joanne hated to call on her because Edna's baby, Oliver, was only two months old. He was a happy, sleepy little guy who looked so much like his daddy, Staff Sergeant Luke Philips, that it made people laugh when they saw them together.

Joanne adored the baby, she'd been able to spoil him a couple of times when Edna needed a babysitter.

"I'd love to," Edna said when Joanne worked up the

nerve to ask her. "Oliver already loves being around kids, and with Susie and Marcus, it's like one big family anyway. When do you need me?"

So, the following morning Joanne drove to Calgary and, feeling both nervous and frightened, pulled into the driveway of the dive bar she used to frequent as a teenager.

Her heart was hammering as she pushed the heavy door of the bar open and searched the room. She saw some old, familiar faces and then she spotted Harper leaning over the pool table.

It felt to Joanne as though she had travelled back in time.

Her friend looked older, but she hadn't changed that much, still in a denim mini-skirt and a black crop top, her ginger hair pulled back in a high ponytail.

As Joanne walked over to her, she noticed the neat whiskey by her side, usual for Harper. And she was evidently still kicking the men's butts in pool by their groaning and cursing.

"Still a pool master, I see," Joanne said, walking up to the fair-skinned woman. Harper considered her for a second, squinting up at her.

"J-bird?" Harper sounded incredulous.

Joanne couldn't help but smile at the nickname. How could they have ever thought it was cool?

"Hi, Harper."

"No freaking way!" Harper laughed and pulled Joanne into a tight hug. "Never thought I'd see you back here, ever again." She pushed Joanne back and held her at arm's length, studying her face. "You look good, girl. Bit tired, bit older. Love the glasses. You still doing the kid thing?"

In their infrequent emails, Joanne had explained about

her divorce, about fostering and running the daycare. But she hadn't yet told Harper about Zalika.

She wished now she'd kept in better touch. She and Harper had been closer than many sisters, back in the day.

"Yeah, got three of 'em now. Latest is a baby from Nigeria."

"Nigeria, huh? Damn, momma. You been busy," Harper gently punched Joanne's shoulder and then wrapped an arm around her and led her towards the bar. "Tequila still your poison?"

"I don't drink as much anymore," Joanne said carefully. Tequila was a part of the life she'd left behind the last time she walked out of here, walked away from Brad. "Besides, I'm driving so..."

"Club soda it is then. Gordon!" she called out to the bartender. "Pour my friend here a dry one."

The two women carried their drinks to the booth that they always used to sit in, way back when.

It was occupied by a couple of men, so Joanne started to move to another one, but Harper grabbed her arm to stop her. She stood in front of the men and with a wave of her hand ordered them to leave. They didn't move.

"Piss off, or I'll dump this slop over your heads," she growled, and they got up, cursing under their breaths.

"I'd forgotten how bossy you are." Joanne slipped into the left side of the table, sliding all the way in to make room. They always used to sit on the same side. But this time Harper sat across from her.

"Yeah, only now I actually have the right to be bossy." Harper sipped on her whiskey. "I bought the place a year ago. It was going under, so the previous owner was selling it dirt cheap to get rid of it."

"Is it doing better now?"

"Not really. But I wanted to give it a try, maybe build up the business. Too many memories in here, you know?"

She gave Joanne a sideways glance. "Brad is helping out a bit to keep 'er afloat. He always asks about you, the one that got away from him."

"Speaking of Brad," Joanne lowered her voice, "do you think you could arrange a meeting for me?"

"Thought you were done with all that," Harper said, not bothering to whisper. "You're not still carrying a torch for him, are you?"

"Absolutely not! I--I just need to ask him for a favor." There'd been a doctor, the one Brad had wanted her to go to. He'd likely falsify Zalika's medical records—for a hefty fee.

"What kinda favor? You know those usually come with a price."

"I know. It's not just about money," Joanne said. She really was willing to do whatever it took. Even blow her entire savings account, such as it was, on some shady doctor if that's what it took.

Harper pushed her drink across the table and moved to Joanne's side.

"You sure you want to get mixed up with him again?" she said, just above a whisper, moving closer to Joanne. "He still carries a torch for you, he's not gonna just say hi and let it go at that. It's dangerous, J-bird."

"It's about one of my kids," Joanne said and explained Zalika's situation to Harper.

"Brad is an ass," she said when Joanne had finished her story. "I think he's probably dealing, he'll want you to do something bad. You don't want to arrange anything through him. I know a doc, he's been good to some of the girls who work here. Let me see if I can get ahold of him. He's good, and he's willing to bend the rules."

"I so appreciate this, Harper," Joanne smiled, and a wave of relief washed over her.

"Those kids are hella lucky to have you for a mom, J-bird," Harper took one of Joanne's hands inside her own. "Not all kids are."

Joanne cupped a hand over the side of Harper's face. She knew Harper had grown up in foster care. And most of her experiences had been far less than ideal. From the little Harper had revealed, she'd lived a nightmare during her teen years.

Harper was actually one of the reasons why Joanne had started fostering. She wanted to give as many kids as possible a positive experience instead of the hellish one Harper had experienced. She leaned over and enveloped her friend in a huge hug.

After a few moments, Harper wiped away a tear that had created a wet trail down her cheek and dug her cell phone out of her purple bra.

"Put your number in here, I'll call you with any news."

"I owe you one," Joanne said, tapping in her number. "You call me if you ever need anything."

"Let's get you and Zalika settled first," Harper said with a wink, and Joanne leaned over and gave her a quick kiss on the cheek.

"Thank you, more than I can ever say."

"I got your back, J-bird, just like always." Harper grinned at her, and for the first time in the last week, Joanne felt cautiously optimistic.

9

———

Joanne drove home and then waited anxiously for the call from Harper.

On the third day, early in the morning, her cell rang.

"Hi, Harper?" Joanne didn't check the number. She was certain it had to be her friend.

"Good morning, Ms. Logan," a polite female voice said back. "It's Linda from the Medical Centre. I'm calling to confirm Zalika's eight A.M. with Dr. Murphy."

"But I...I didn't think I had--" Joanne hurried to check the fridge door where she wrote appointments down on a magnetic notepad. "We don't have an appointment," she said after she'd checked twice.

"It says here it was booked last night. Dr. Murphy signed it. Have you not spoken to him?"

Not in over a week. Not since that terrible morning, Joanne thought to herself. What could he want with her after that debacle? Her face flamed just thinking of it. But he was Zalika's doctor. She had to go.

"We'll be there," Joanne said. Her little herd would have

to come with, but she knew that they had a play area at the medical center. A quick call to Timothy saying she'd be late, and they were on their way.

Joanne was at the Clinic and had everyone settled with ten minutes to spare. Her stomach was churning with nerves. She dreaded seeing Colin again, and her heart hammered as the nurse ushered her and Zalika into the exam room.

Colin came in a moment later and closed the door behind him.

Joanne looked straight at him, afraid of what he'd say, ashamed of what she'd asked him to do. She opened her mouth to apologize, but he said, "You went looking for a shady doctor, Joanne?"

"How-how did you know?"

"Ahhh, just that he was trying to access Zalika's case history, and of course, I was notified because I'm her primary physician at the moment."

She couldn't read the expression in his lovely blue eyes.

He looked at her and shook his head, making his dark hair tumble over his forehead. He shoved it away with an impatient gesture.

"I understand you're desperate, but if you get caught falsifying documents you will not only be losing Zalika." His voice was soft, but there was no mistaking the assurance in his voice.

Joanne was barely breathing, trying to hold in the fear and pain. And the shame of having dragged Colin into this.

"Please, sit down." Colin motioned her to take a seat.

He took Zalika and set her gently down on a blanket on the floor and handed her a plastic toy. Then he moved the other chair closer to Joanne's and sat down himself.

"I did some digging," he began. "And I found that they

haven't approved Zalika's adoption yet for financial reasons."

"I—I don't understand."

"You see, dear one, they don't think you can afford to raise another child, especially one that has health issues and may require many more potentially costly treatments."

"But...what?" She struggled to make sense of this new disaster. "They're just going to send her back to Nigeria where that treatment is not even readily available to her?" Joanne felt tears threatening.

"No," Colin said softly and took her hands in his. "They're looking for someone more suitable to adopt her. Before her Visa expires."

"What?" Joanne pulled her hands out of his reach. She leaned down and picked her baby up, holding her tight. "That's ridiculous. I'm her *mother,* she can't go to someone new. How do you even know all that?"

"I have a friend who works with the adoption agency." Colin got up, and Joanne took a step back.

"And can't that friend do anything about this?" she asked, the tears welling up again. *"Please,* Colin. Please?" Here she was begging him again.

"No, that's not how it works," Colin said. "But maybe there's something *we* could do."

Joanne stared at him, waiting.

"If you were..." Colin started, but he paused. "If you were married, your husband's income would be counted in too."

"Oh, I just need to find a husband then, no big deal," Joanne said through the tears now pouring down her cheeks. "Do you think they'll have any organic ones at the market?"

She was almost hysterical now.

Zalika was looking at her mother, her little forehead

wrinkled in confusion, her face crumbling up to cry. She turned her big, inquisitive eyes to Colin, who threw her a reassuring smile, before turning his attention back to Joanne.

"Joanne, I was thinking," he began, but three soft knocks cut him off. The young nurse opened the door slightly and peeked her head inside.

"Doctor, your 8:30 is getting a little restless," she smiled.

"We're done here anyway," Joanne said and started for the door. Colin grabbed her arm to stop her.

"I'll just be another couple of wee minutes," he told the nurse, who nodded and closed the door. "Joanne," he blurted. "You can marry me. I have a steady job with a decent income and having a pediatric surgeon as a husband is definitely going to help your case."

Joanne's mouth dropped open, and she stared at Colin. "M—*marry* you? But—but you barely know me. I—I barely know you."

Colin shook his head, and words poured out of him. "I know everything about you that's important, Joanne. I know you're kind and generous and loving. I know that you're beautiful and sexy and funny. We'd have plenty of time to get to know one another after we were married. And you said you were willing to do anything."

"And you said you *weren't*."

"I said I wasn't willing to lose my job. And I'm still not."

"But a fake marriage is okay? Because---because it *isn't*, not to me!"

"That's not all it would be. Listen, Joanne, I—"

"You have a patient waiting," Joanne said.

She opened the door and ran to the kid's play area, collected her other two and drove to work, feeling as though she was in shock. He couldn't possibly be serious about getting married, just like that.

Could he?

She worked at the daycare, then after work busied herself with her kids and the mounds of laundry that always needed to be done.

Colin called numerous times, and she ignored the phone.

After dinner, she took the kids out for ice cream and then to the park, leaving her phone at home. When she came home, she bathed her kids and put them to bed, one by one.

It was way past midnight and a couple of glasses of wine later when she looked at her phone again.

She'd missed countless calls and text messages from Colin, but those weren't the only ones. She also had a couple from Harper.

Doctor on board but gonna cost you big time.

And from Colin, *Joanne, please, please let's talk about this. Don't do anything rash.*

Joanne texted Harper back. She simply couldn't deal with Colin right now.

10

"You sure about this, J-bird?"

Harper sat in the booth across from Joanne, forehead creased with concern.

Joanne had driven to Calgary early that morning and they'd met in the little café where they used to have breakfast.

"Why do you keep asking me that?" Joanne turned her head towards the younger woman who didn't meet her gaze. "*You're* still doing business with Brad."

"Yeah, but I'm a low-life with no family. You got kids."

"Don't talk about yourself that way, you're no low life. And with the kids, I'm going to have Zalika taken from me unless I come into some money fast."

She'd told Harper about Colin's incredible offer.

She'd thought of little else since she'd last seen him. It was so preposterous she could hardly get her head around it. And it hurt that he'd make an offer like that out of pity. What else could it be?

Harper shook her head. "You don't want to borrow anything from Brad, Joanne. Trust me on this."

"I don't have a choice. I went to the bank, they turned me down."

"But you *do*, though! Have a choice. Why not take that doctor guy up on his offer?"

"I don't want to be indebted to him for the rest of my life," Joanne said, staring out at the busy street. "I don't want to marry someone I barely know. One bad marriage is enough for a lifetime."

"Better marriage than Brad," Harper shot back.

Joanne looked at the address Harper had given her.

It was in one of the posh areas of Calgary. Brad had said he'd meet her there in an hour. He'd obviously made money on whatever it was he was doing.

"You're right," Joanne started in a harsh tone, "I totally don't want to be involved in any way with Brad. But it's either that or lose my precious baby."

She got up, heading towards what was bound to be the biggest mistake of her life.

11

———

When Colin finished his early shift, he hurried to the daycare to find Joanne.

He'd gone about everything the wrong way. When he had another chance, he'd go about it differently, and he was determined to find the right opportunity to try again.

"She took the afternoon off," Timothy said. "She was heading up to the Ferguson farm with the kids."

Colin drove fast up the valley road. He was going to track her down, he couldn't let it go another day.

She'd refused to answer his calls, and when he went to her house she either wasn't there or refused to answer the door.

He pulled into Ferguson's driveway and hurried to the door.

"Dr. Murphy?" Edna stared at him, her arms full of babies. She had Zalika on one hip and her son on the other. "Is something wrong?"

"Nothing's wrong. I was looking for Joanne. I take it she's not around?" Colin tried to hide his panic.

Edna looked confused. "She said she had an appointment in Calgary. She dropped Lily and Alex off about three hours ago."

"Damnation," Colin breathed. "Can you please call her? If she sees your number, maybe she'll pick up. She won't answer my calls."

"Why would she not pick up *your* calls?" Edna asked. "Please come in, Doctor. I'll get my cell; it's in the kitchen."

Colin waited with growing impatience as Edna punched in Joanne's number.

"It's gone to voice mail, Doctor."

"Keep trying, please. It's a matter of extreme urgency," he said and took one of his business cards out of his pocket. "Call me immediately if you get hold of her."

He'd checked, and the crooked doctor that Joanne had been looking to contact lived in Calgary. Because of the financial issues, Zalika's future with Joanne was more complicated than just a Visa.

He got back into his car and banged his hands on the steering wheel, not knowing what to do or where to go next.

He took his phone out and called her for the hundredth time. But this time, she answered.

"Joanne? Joanne, where are you?"

"Are you Joanne's doctor friend?" he heard an unfamiliar female voice ask.

"Who is this? Where's Joanne?"

"Are you him? Are you Colin?" the woman persisted.

"Yes! Yes, I am. Who-"

"You need to stop Joanne." She sounded frantic.

"Stop her from what? Where is she?"

"Calgary. Here in Calgary. She's about to make a really big mistake."

"*Calgary*? That's two and a half hours away." Colin felt panicked. "I can't get there for two and a half hours."

"Damn. That's gonna be too late."

"Can you not stop her? Whatever it is she's about to do, you have to stop her."

"I can't. I tried. She won't listen to me."

"What's your name?"

"Harper."

"Harper. How do you know Joanne? And how do you happen to have her phone?"

"She's an old friend of mine. Her phone was out of juice, so I loaned her mine. I've just plugged hers into my car charger."

"Look, Harper. I can't possibly get there in time, so you'll need to be the one to help our friend. Please!"

"I don't see what I can do. She's pigheaded stubborn, that girl." There was both caring and panic in her tone.

"Listen, Harper. You go to Joanne, wherever she is, and you tell her that Edna called. Edna's minding her kids. You tell her that something's up and she needs to call Edna immediately. You understand?"

There was silence from the other end.

"Harper?"

"Okay, okay. I'll try."

"A mother's instincts are powerful, but they are *not* always right. It would be best if you stopped her from making this big mistake, Harper," Colin pleaded.

"Okay, already, I'll go." It was the last thing Colin heard before the line went dead.

He was still just outside Edna's farm, so he made a sharp U-turn and drove back into her driveway as a police car pulled in just behind him.

"Hi, doc. Something wrong with the kids?" Luke Philips looked concerned. "Or Edna?"

"Your family is fine; I'm here on another matter."

"Well then, come on in." Luke headed for the door, and Colin followed.

"Here's your daddy, and not a moment too soon. I need to change a little girl's diaper." Edna handed Luke his son just as her phone started ringing.

"It's Joanne," Edna said, checking the display.

"Wait! Don't answer just yet, please." Colin grabbed the phone from her hands.

"What's going on, doc?" Luke gave Colin a puzzled look.

"I'll explain everything," he said, "but right now, I need Edna to tell Joanne that Lily's been sick a couple of times and that she's asking for her. Please, Edna. Joanne's about to make a terrible mistake."

Edna looked at Luke. He studied Colin for an instant and then nodded at his wife. "Do as he asks, love."

After getting the go-ahead nod from her husband, Edna answered the phone and repeated what Colin had said.

Colin could hear Joanne's panicked voice through the phone, asking Edna to call him and take Lily to the hospital if need be, saying she was heading back immediately.

Colin knew Joanne would be furious at him for putting her through hell until she got back to Starwood.

But he also knew that an emergency with one of her kids was the only way to prevent her from making a grave mistake.

Luke and Edna were asking him questions, and Colin wasn't sure what he would say. He didn't want to get Joanne into more trouble than she might already have accomplished on her own.

He prayed Harper had gotten to her in time.

12

"So exactly what's going on, Doctor?" Luke's tone demanded an answer.

Colin could only tell them of the problems Joanne was having with Zalika's Visa. The rest was private, to be settled between him and Joanne.

"But that's horrible," Edna exclaimed when he was done. "Joanne just said that she had a business meeting in Calgary, she didn't tell me about the Visa thing. But why did you say Lily was ill? Why must she come back so quickly?"

Colin hesitated. "She's really angry with me at the moment and won't answer my calls. But I have a solution to the problems with Zalika if only I can get her to listen."

"You care for her," Edna said slowly, studying his face.

"Very much." Colin felt his ears turning red.

"She needs *someone* to care for her," Edna stated. "She's so alone."

Luke nodded. "We think a great deal of Joanne. Just let us know if there's anything we can do to help."

At Colin's request, both Luke and Edna promised to keep everything that Colin had confided just between the three of them, and Luke urged Colin to come to him privately if Joanne was in trouble and he'd figure something out.

"Joanne will be coming straight here. Do you mind if I sit outside and wait?" Colin asked.

"Outside? Absolutely not, you'll sit right here in my kitchen and have coffee while we both wait for her," Edna insisted.

It seemed as if an eternity passed before Joanne's car came speeding down the driveway. Moments later, she was at the door.

"You go to her, Colin," Edna insisted. "I'll just be in the other room with these rascals." She scooped up Zalika and Oliver and disappeared.

Joanne's hazel eyes were huge and frightened behind her glasses, and she took a step back when Colin opened the door.

"Colin? Omigod, is—is Lily alright? What's the matter with her? Is that why you're here?"

"Lily's absolutely fine," Colin said, looking straight into her eyes. "She's playing with Susie out back of the house. Can we please talk, Joanne?"

He led the way into the kitchen and pulled out a chair.

Joanne plopped into it as if all her energy had evaporated. And as she sat down, she let out a huge sigh of relief, and tears started flowing down her cheeks.

Colin took a deep breath and sent up a silent prayer for help.

"It was totally my idea to have Edna suggest that Lily was ill, and I apologize for giving you cause to worry. You see, your friend Harper called me, asking if I could keep you from making a terrible mistake."

He sat down near Joanne. Nervous, he let moments of

silence slide past while studying Joanne and giving her time to compose herself.

"I can't believe that you'd scare me this way," she said in a quivery voice. "How could you *do* that to me?" She started to get up, but Colin grabbed her arm.

"This time you are going to hear me out, Joanne."

"Let go of me." She glared at him.

"I---love----you." He released her arm, hoping against hope that the declaration was enough to keep her rooted in place.

"I think I've loved you ever since I met you in the hospital when Zalika had her surgery. You're the reason I took the job here in Starwood, in hopes that you'd go out with me. I know you don't feel the same about me, but I'm asking—I'm begging you---to just give me a chance to court you. I'm sure I can convince you that I'm really not a bad sort of bloke when you get to know me."

"Oh, Colin." Like a punctured balloon, Joanne sank back into her chair. "It's not about you. It's me. There's so much about me you don't know. If you knew everything about me, you'd head straight back to Calgary."

"Then tell me. I promise you It won't change the way I feel, nothing could do that."

She stared at him and shook her head. "It will though." There was agony in her tone. "I--I made a terrible mistake when I was young. I got pregnant with a no-good guy, and he wanted me to have an abortion. I did it, and since then I've lost three other babies, the last one full term, a little girl stillborn."

With that painful information out in the open tears began running down her face again and she took off her glasses and swiped her cheeks with the back of her hand. "Her--her name was Angelina. It wrecked my marriage, losing those babies. I was depressed for a long time. I still think losing my babies was punishment for the abortion."

"Ahhhh, sweetheart. Not so, not so at all." Colin dug in his pockets and pulled out a fistful of crumbled tissues, handing them to her. "See, my sweet lass, the God I believe in is love and only love. There would never be retribution for a mistake. And that's all it was, sweetheart; a mistake. Made by a young girl who meant no harm."

Joanne looked into his blue eyes, wishing she could believe him. "But the fact is, I probably will *never* be able to have babies, Colin. And most men want kids of their own, my ex-husband did. I've made a life for myself with my foster kids, I want to adopt them." She sniffed and blew her nose. "I'm just not any good at adult relationships."

"And isn't that what I'm saying, that I can help you with the wee ones? Seeing you make a horrible, illegal-type mistake, lose yet another child, possibly all three, is the last thing I want, and for the record, I'm not the sort to want only my own progeny," he continued. "But I didn't ask you to marry me only for the sake of the children. I love *you*, Joanne, and I truly do want to spend the rest of my life with you, be a father to all of your children. If we can't have our own, there are plenty more precious wee ones needing a home."

Joanne's heart was racing, and she felt her hands trembling as Colin's sincerity registered. But she had to be absolutely certain. So much was at stake.

"Why would you love a shell of a human being? I feel as if something's broken in me, something that might never mend."

He shook his head. "I've seen broken. You're not it. You are one of the strongest people I know, Joanne." He placed a hand on her tightly clasped fists. "I saw you when Zalika was struggling to live. You were the one who loved her into fighting for life."

He looked deep into her eyes. "You've pushed past pain, and now you're changing the lives of three little children, and one grown man if you will, giving Lily, Alex and Zalika all the love they could ever need in life. Love they could not get anywhere else. And I want to be a part of that, dear one."

"You're absolutely certain about this?" She looked up into his eyes, and his sincerity was crystal clear.

"I am, as certain as I've been about anything."

It tool long moments before Joanne nodded.

This would be a big step, a leap of faith, but somehow it was beginning to feel right.

She got up and walked over to her bag. She pulled out her phone, called someone and put it to her ear.

Colin studied her face, trying to figure out what was going on.

"Mrs. White? It's Joanne Logan," she said. "I've been told that Social Services are looking for another family to foster Zalika. Yes, financial reasons, I know... Yes... Well, I need you to delay the process if you could. I'll explain soon. Just, please, can you give me a week? Thank you, Mrs. White. I'll call you back this evening and explain. Thank you again....bye now."

Colin had the stupidest, sweetest smile on his face when she turned to look at him.

She walked back to him slowly and stood mere inches in front of him. "You didn't actually ever ask me," she said, looking into his eyes. "You've never really asked me to marry you. You said that I *could* marry you, but never asked the question. So, if you truly mean it, then ask," she demanded.

He put his hands on her shoulders. "Joanne Logan, will you be my wife?"

"I will," she said. And in a shy whisper, she added, "And you've never kissed me, either."

He drew her into his arms and bent his head. The kiss felt like it had been years in the making. Not just on his part, but hers too.

There was passion and need, and a sweet tenderness that touched her to the depths of her soul.

There was a rightness to it, a feeling of security, promise and of coming home after a long, arduous journey.

13

They were married four days later in the field behind the Ferguson farm, on a soft early fall day when the leaves had turned golden and the air was filled with birdsong.

Colin had learned that B.C. was one of the easiest provinces in which to get married. There was no mandatory waiting period and a license was available immediately, as long as identification was produced and a hundred-dollar fee paid.

"Do you, Joanne Logan, take this man—" Barbara Columbine's husky melodic voice easily reached the twenty-three guests seated on the folding chairs Edna had borrowed from the senior citizen's retirement home.

Barbara was a local minister and a wedding officiant, a native of Starwood greatly in demand for unorthodox marriages such as this one. Quirky, professional and wildly attractive at sixty something, she'd been delighted to include the children in the ceremony.

Colin, breathtakingly handsome in a grey suit and white

dress shirt, held Zalika. There was a dark stain on his silver tie where the baby had upchucked on him.

Lily and Alex, hand in hand, stood just in front of the bridal couple.

As the vows were exchanged, they joined in with a hearty "We do, too."

Edna and Kate had insisted on a proper wedding, with a luncheon afterwards at the Truckstop.

Luke was Colin's best man, and Edna stood beside Joanne as maid of honor.

Joanne had asked Harper to stand up for her, but her friend had been unable to attend.

"I'm so, so sorry, J-bird," Harper had said on the phone. "There's stuff going on here and I just can't get away on such short notice. I'm so glad you're not mad at me, and I couldn't be happier for you. And I'll come and visit real soon."

Joanne made her promise.

In retrospect, Harper had done her a huge favor by telling Colin what was going on that day. She shuddered every time she thought of what might have happened if Harper's call hadn't come before she got to Brad's house.

In spite of the short notice and the hasty preparation, everything went off wonderfully well for a Starwood wedding.

Edna's latest puppy, Garfield, got out of the house during the ceremony, barking and jumping on the kids, licking the minister's legs, peeing on Colin's shoes and reducing everyone to helpless giggles, until Edna regained control of him.

Mac and Edna's mother, Dixie Ferguson, who had Alzheimer's, stood up in the middle of the ceremony and began to sing, "Row, row, row your boat, gently down the stream."

She had a lovely soprano voice, Joanne thought.

Barbara Columbine smiled and waited, and when Dixie was finished, thanked her and gave an impromptu little talk on how meaningful the song was, that far too often people tried rowing *up* the stream instead of down.

And then the ceremony was over.

She was Colin's wife.

He took Joanne in his arms and kissed her thoroughly and reverently.

She didn't tell him that his cuff links didn't match and that his socks were inside out. Now that she'd made the decision to be his partner, she could only see how endearing he was, how infinitely kind and generous, how easy he would be to love.

"Once everything's in order, we'll have an outright *feast* to celebrate," Colin promised Joanne. "We'll invite the whole damn town!"

"He's a keeper," Edna whispered into Joanne's ear.

He truly was.

Joanne felt blessed, as if the entire day was a dream. She also knew that she wouldn't be able to really celebrate fully until Zalika, as well as Lily and Alex, were officially hers.

Or rather, *theirs*. The kids, all three of them, already were at ease with their new foster dad.

Colin had spent every spare moment the past few days getting to know them, getting to know Joanne better as well.

He had a way with kids.

He also had a way with her. Joanne blushed, remembering the previous evening. The kids were in bed and she and Colin were relaxing with a glass of wine.

"There's something we need to discuss," he'd said.

They were sitting close together on the sofa. His arm was around her shoulder. She liked being close to him, liked his warmth, his smell of antiseptic soap and the clean, woodsy scent that was just Colin.

"There hasn't been time to romance you the way I want to do," he began in a soft voice. "We'll be legally married tomorrow, but I want you to know I'll not rush you, Joanne. I'll sleep here on the sofa until you're ready."

He turned her head with a gentle hand and kissed her, long and passionately. "I want you, you know that. But I'll wait as long as you want, absolutely no pressure."

The way he made her feel, that wait would be a very short one. Hours, instead of days.

14

─────────

Three weeks after the wedding, Colin and Joanne walked into the building that housed Social Services.

Zalika was in Joanne's arms, Lily in Colin's.

The little girl had fallen heavily for her new dad, and she had him pretty much wrapped around her little finger.

Alex walked between them, holding their free hands.

Mrs. White was waiting for them and the look in her eyes when she saw them said it all. She had a big smile plastered across her face, and if Joanne didn't know any better, she'd say the social worker was a bit teary-eyed too.

"Good news," Mrs. White said, without any preliminary chit-chat. She knew the verdict was what they needed to hear.

"The government has decided to renew Zalika's Visa, and the agency is not looking at moving her at this time."

"Oh, thank goodness. Oh, I'm so relieved." Joanne's tears were joyful, and Colin cheered, then thrust a fist into the air in a victory salute.

They all knew that this wasn't an ending. There would

be the first of many hearings. There would be a lot of unannounced visits as well. This time the agency would be scrutinizing Joanne as a wife as well as a mother.

Well, she thought, let them go right ahead. She knew she was a good mother. It was one area of her life that she was totally confident about.

They'd also be trying to make sure that her marriage to Colin was not a sham, and Joanne hoped that they would soon decide the marriage was solid.

She couldn't believe how deliciously happy she and Colin were. They truly were well suited, and she could say honestly now that she loved him, a love that grew stronger each and every day. There was still a tiny part of her that thought Colin was too good to be true, that rep waiting for the other shoe to drop. She fought it, but the insecurity was there.

Joanne shoved her doubts away. All that really mattered at this moment was that the agency had stopped looking into other foster families for Zalika and that her temporary Visa was renewed.

The adoptions were a hurdle they'd cross when the time came.

They'd have to take it one day at a time, and that was tough, because she wanted certainty. She wanted the security of knowing her family was safe, together, not at the mercy of outside influences. But only time could make that happen.

As they left the agency and climbed into the new van Colin had bought to hold his new family, Joanne's cell rang.

15

"Hi, Harper. What's up? Are you coming for that promised visit? I've been trying to get hold of you for two weeks now."

Joanne had wondered why her friend hadn't answered her texts or her calls.

"J-bird, I—I need a huge favor." Harper's shaky voice echoed through the receiver. She sounded scared. "I'm at the Starwood Bus Station. Do you—do you think you could pick me up?" Harper's voice cracked, and Joanne knew her friend was sobbing.

"Of course," Joanne said, doing her best to mask her concern. "Sit tight, sweetie, we'll be there in a few minutes."

"What's wrong?" Colin asked as soon as he caught a glimpse of Joanne's face.

"Something bad is up with Harper, something terrible by the way she sounds. I need to go get her, she's at the bus station, she's scared and she's crying." Joanne looked around at the car, loaded with children and toys and diaper bags, wondering anxiously where they'd even fit Harper in.

"We'll drive home, you can grab *your* car from there,"

Colin suggested. "Then I'll take this lot to the park for a while, and you and Harper can meet us there afterwards or if that's not good, I'll bring the kids home. Take your time, sounds like she needs you."

"Thank you. Thank you, Colin."

She still wasn't used to having help with emergencies. Colin truly, absolutely, was a fine man. How had she gotten so lucky? How could she have any lingering doubts?

It took only moments to retrieve her car and blow goodbye kisses to the kids. She planted a huge, grateful kiss on Colin's lips. Then she drove to the bus station, parked, and hurried into the small waiting area.

Harper was leaning on the wall. She had her back to Joanne, her arms hugging her body, a fat blue suitcase at her feet.

Joanne hurried toward her. Something felt very wrong. Harper seemed to be huddled into herself, shoulders hunched, hoodie hiding her face.

"Hey, you," she said, gently touching Harper's shoulder.

Harper cried out and whirled around, giving Joanne just enough time to see the purple and black bruises before she fell into Joanne's arms, sobbing and shaking.

"Hey, easy does it." Joanne held her, patting her back the way she did with the kids when they needed soothing.

The dark glasses slipped off, and Joanne grabbed them and tucked them in her jacket pocket. She let Harper cry for as long as she needed, holding her in her arms.

"What's happened?" she asked once Harper quieted. Joanne could guess, though. This had something to do with Brad.

"I need help," Harper croaked. "Oh, J-bird, I'm in such bad trouble."

Joanne reached over, tracing the outline of the purple

bruise around Harper's left eye, brushing away the new tears that were streaming down her smashed-up face.

"You've come to the right place," Joanne said gently. "We specialize in trouble, Colin and I. Let's go home, and you can tell me all about it."

Joanne picked up the suitcase, her arm protectively around her friend.

Harper was still leaning on her, still sobbing and shaking so hard she staggered when she tried to walk.

Joanne set the case down and waited, patting her back, and holding her up. She felt rage, hot and red, towards whoever had done this to her friend. She'd never seen her strong, capable, confident Harper so vulnerable, so defeated. So terrified.

"What are you so afraid of, love? You're safe here, I promise."

"I need help," was all Harper mumbled again. "I—I didn't know where else to go. But I don't want to bring trouble down on you and your family."

"You did exactly the right thing, coming to us," Joanne assured her. She reached over, tracing the outline of the ugly bruise around Harper's left eye, brushing away the new tears that were streaming down her battered face. "You're like a sister to me, Harper. You're my family, I love you dearly. You've come to the right place," Joanne said quietly. "Let's go home, and you can tell me all about it."

Joanne picked up the suitcase again, her arm protectively around her friend, leading the way over to her car.

She did her best to conceal the shock and utter horror she felt at how battered Harper was, how terrified and how injured. How could she best help her?

Colin would know. She no longer had to figure everything out on her own, she reminded herself. And because of him, she'd learned in the past few weeks that there was a solution to everything, no matter how desperate it seemed at the time.

Colin had taught her that, her strong, loving husband, whose huge, generous heart seemed to have room for everyone. She knew without even questioning that he, too, would do whatever he could to help Harper. To keep her safe.

For the first time in her life, Joanne wasn't alone, and with that realization, her heart overflowed with love for the man who'd rescued her, who loved her, loved her babies and supported her totally. How had she ever gotten so lucky?

She'd also had good friends who'd been there for her, as she would be for Harper.

But Harper still held back, shaking her head, eyes wild. "I can't go to your house, J-bird. Look at me, that nice guy you married will take one look and—"

"He'll take one look and do whatever he can to help. We're a team, Colin and I."

"But what if *he* comes after me? I'm so scared I'll put you and your family at risk."

Joanne sensed that *he* was Brad, and at that moment she wanted to kill him herself.

"It's safe here, we'll deal with whatever happens. You'll be fine, we all will be. Please, sweetie, get in the car. Let's go home now." She opened the car door, half supporting Harper as she collapsed onto the passenger seat.

Joanne tossed the suitcase into the back.

The agonized moan Harper tried to smother as she struggled into the car told Joanne that the injuries went much further, much deeper, more serious, than black eyes and bruises. Harper was in severe pain.

Joanne hurried around to the driver's side, got in and started the car, then hesitated before pulling out.

"Harper, sweetie, you're hurt really bad. Are you sure we shouldn't go to the medical centre, get you looked at? Colin will—"

"*Nooooo*," Harper shrieked. "*Nooooo,* I can't, let me out, I can't—"

"Okay, okay, just take deep breaths. No medical centre, we'll just go home. Hush now, just relax." Joanne reached over and grabbed Harper's arm, scared that her friend would jump out of the car, scared too that she was badly injured internally.

Colin would help. He was a doctor, he'd tend to Harper. Joanne was trying not to panic. "Please trust me, my dear friend."

Joanne pulled onto the street, and turned at the corner, taking the shortest, fastest route home. "The one thing I've learned is that no matter how horrible things seem at the time, there's always a solution. Colin's taught me that."

The words were meant for Harper, but Joanne realized they were also meant for her. To remind her that trust was something she'd never had before with a man.

She'd never before trusted anyone the way she did Colin. She realized for the first time that she truly *did* trust him, unconditionally.

These past weeks had been joyful and exciting, but there was always the constant underlying strain of whether Zalika's passport would be renewed, and whether or not social services would leave Zalika with her and Colin. She hadn't had time yet to really take in the wonderful news they'd had today.

And also, Joanne admitted now, she'd held back a little from believing she could be happy. She hadn't been able to fully trust, even in herself, trust that she deserved happiness and love, or let herself accept that she was worthwhile, that the wonderful things that were happening for her wouldn't be snatched away.

I do deserve it. I'm worth it. And I'm so grateful.

It had taken this, seeing Harper this way, reminding her of what her life might have been. What her life *would* have been if she hadn't had the courage to change it.

She pulled up in front of the cottage. Colin's van wasn't back yet. He was giving her time, the way he gave her everything she needed.

"We're home, honey. Let's go in and have a cup of tea."

Small things. New beginnings. Maybe not happy ever after, because life wasn't like that.

But for today, there was friendship and children, and safety and hope.

And love. Joanne's heart overflowed with love, for her wonderful husband, the children she adored, the terrified, battered friend beside her.

For today, that was more than enough.

*****

AFTERWORD

Starwood is a little coal mining town deep in the Canadian Rockies where romance flourishes, intrigue abounds and lives are never as simple as they seem.

Starwood is the setting for **Starwood Chronicles,** a series of short exciting romantic reads about the fun people who lead their lives in a valley, in the shadow of the Rocky Mountains.

The books in the series are:

Biggest Little Truckstop
Every Little Thing
Biggest Little Mustache
Biggest Little Heart
Biggest Little Secret

Bobby says:

I was born and grew up in this little Rocky Mountain coal mining town of Sparwood, B.C., Canada. Our big claim to fame is THE BIG TRUCK, advertised as the world's largest, parked on a lot right when you come into town.

I always wanted to start a restaurant near it and call it the Biggest Little Truckstop In The World.

Well, we all know what the failure rate is with restaurants, so instead, I decided to write a series of romances about an imaginary town called Starwood.

Here's a picture of the truck, thanks to my sister Karen.

That's me in the white jacket down by the wheel.

ALSO BY BOBBY HUTCHINSON

<u>STARWOOD CHRONICLES</u>

Biggest Little Truckstop

Every Little Thing

Biggest Little Mustache

Biggest Little Heart

Biggest Little Secret

<u>MEDICAL ROMANCE</u>

Drastic Measures

Full Recovery

Double Jeopardy

Picking Clover,

Nursing the Doctor

Patient Care

The Baby Doctor

Acute Care

A Past And Present Love

Love To The Rescue

One Little Miracle

Healer

<u>WESTERN PRAIRIE BRIDES</u>

<u>(Historical Romance)</u>

Lantern In The Window

Silent Light, Silent Love

Medicine Woman

Western Prairie Brides Box Set

Rose's Maile Order Brides And Grooms

Darling Clementine

Tangled Lives

ABOUT THE AUTHOR

Bobby Hutchinson lives, breathes, reads and writes books. She lives in a small city in the Rocky Mountains of B.C., Canada, a little larger version of Starwood.

She isn't an RCMP officer, she doesn't waitress anymore, she's never shot a stalker-but some of her wonderful female friends have done (most) of the above, which made for fantastic research in Biggest Little Mustache.

Her favorite quote is, "When you change the way you look at a thing, the thing you look at changes."

You can always reach her by email:
bobbyhut@telus.net